OH, BROTHER!

Adapted by Jasmine Jones
Based on the series created by Terri Minsky
Part One is based on a teleplay written
by Douglas Tuber & Tim Maile.
Part Two is based on a teleplay written
by Bob Thomas.

Watch it on

Disney CHANNEL

abc Kids

Disney PRESS

VOLO

New York

Lizzie McGuire

PART ONE

CHAPTER ONE

Lizzie McGuire was sitting at the kitchen table, struggling to write her history report. Why do we even have to learn about this stuff? Lizzie wondered as she took notes on the chapter. I mean, it's all totally over.

And speaking of totally over . . . Lizzie thought as she watched her brother Matt practicing his latest magic trick. He was flapping a scarf. After a minute, it turned into a cane. Lizzie rolled her eyes.

Ever since Gammy McGuire sent Matt a

magic kit for his birthday, he had been going crazy with the tricks. And he was driving everyone else crazy, too. Well . . . everyone except for Mom and Dad, Lizzie realized, watching her parents as they calmly sliced vegetables for dinner. So I guess that only leaves me, she thought. But still—isn't that enough?

"Wow!" Matt said as he stared at his cane. "That was amazing. Hey, Lizzie, you wanna see a magic trick?"

Lizzie looked down at her paper. "No."

"For my next illusion," Matt announced, completely ignoring Lizzie's wishes, "the famous Floating Ball . . ." So, Matt was making a grapefruit-sized silver ball float around under a scarf, Lizzie thought. Big deal. Dad makes a real grapefruit disappear every morning at breakfast.

"It floats on top of the scarf! It hides

behind the scarf! It zooms through the air!" Matt announced.

The ball flew forward and conked Lizzie on the head. "Ow!" she cried, grabbing the ball and scarf and chucking them into the garbage. "It flies into the trash!" she shouted.

"Dad," Matt whined, "Lizzie threw my trick away!"

"Lizzie, don't throw your brother's trick away," Mr. McGuire said in a bored voice as he kept on slicing and dicing.

Matt flashed Lizzie an evil grin. "Ha!" He fished the ball out of the wastebasket and carried it triumphantly to Lizzie. He thrust it into her face. "Now, kiss it and say you're sorry," Matt commanded.

Lizzie shoved the ball away. "Get out of my face, cactus-head."

"Mom, Lizzie called me cactus-head!" Matt complained.

"Lizzie, don't call your brother a cactus-head," Mrs. McGuire said automatically.

Fine—he's a cactus-*brain*, Lizzie thought. "But I'm trying to do my homework and he won't stop bothering me with his stupid magic tricks," Lizzie cried.

"They're *not* stupid," Matt insisted as he pulled a deck of cards from his magic kit. "Here, pick a card—" He fanned the deck in her face.

Matt has got to stop getting all up in my face, Lizzie thought. Furious, she took a card and slipped it into her pocket. There, she thought, whine about that.

Sure enough. "Liz-zie!" Matt wailed.

"Liz-zie!" his sister repeated in a mocking tone.

"Kids. . . ." Mrs. McGuire said in a warning voice.

Matt reached for the card, but Lizzie held it

away from him. "I need the card to do the trick!" Matt insisted.

"I can do a better one with it—" Lizzie snapped. She slipped the card out of her pocket and tore it up. "Ta-da!" she said, tossing the shredded card into the air. "I turned it into confetti!"

Matt glared at her. "Well, well," he said, "how about I turn *this* into confetti—" Matt yanked a pink scarf out of his sleeve.

"That's mine!" Lizzie cried. "And I told you to stop going into my closet!"

"It wasn't in your closet," Matt said in his most annoying know-it-all voice. "It was in your underwear drawer."

"That's it," Lizzie said through clenched teeth. She grabbed Matt's shirt and yanked him forward. "I'm telling Dad what *really* happened to his sunglasses."

"Fine," Matt said smoothly. "I'll tell Mom

what you were talking to Miranda about on the phone last night. At *eleven-thirty*," he added, putting extra emphasis on the way-past-lights-out time. "Ooooh," Matt squealed, mocking Lizzie's voice, "Ethan Craft is soooo cute. I just want to hug and kiss him all day long!"

Lizzie flashed him the Look of Death, then lunged at him. Matt dodged away, squealing like a stuck pig, and Lizzie chased after him.

"Aaaaaaaagghhhh!" Matt shouted as Lizzie finally grabbed him.

"FREEZE!" Mrs. McGuire shouted.

Lizzie stared at her mother. Then she looked down at Matt. Okay, so this looks kind of bad, Lizzie realized as she stood there, holding Matt upside down by the ankles.

"Let go of me!" Matt shouted, flailing like a cat that had fallen into a toilet bowl.

"Lizzie," Mr. McGuire said slowly, "put

Matt down and step away from your brother."

Lizzie set Matt down and took a giant step away from him. "He started it!" she shouted, just as Matt shouted the same thing, only about Lizzie.

Grrr, Lizzie thought, glaring at her little brother.

"I don't care who started it!" Mrs. McGuire snapped. "You kids have got to stop this constant bickering."

"What is it with you guys?" Lizzie's dad demanded. "You never used to fight like this when you were younger."

That's because Matt didn't know how to talk, Lizzie thought sulkily.

"You used to really take care of each other," Mr. McGuire pointed out. "And that's what a family is—people who love each other and take care of each other."

Lizzie sighed. Her father had a point. She

forced herself to smile and slung her arm around Matt, who squirmed. That's okay, Lizzie thought generously, I can forgive him. "You're right, Dad," Lizzie said sincerely. "Sorry, Mom."

Dad's right. Matt's family. We've gotta have each other's backs. We've gotta be all about love.

Besides, Lizzie thought as she tightened her grip on her brother, it's not like Matt really did anything so horrible.

Except go in my underwear drawer . . . !

On the other hand, the little rat STOLE MY SCARF!

"She's pinching me!" Matt griped.

"He's standing on my foot!" Lizzie cried.

"Well, at least you're not standing on *my* foot," Matt shot back, "you weigh a ton!"

"Oh you little weasel—" Lizzie growled, "I'll teach you to make fun of me!"

"You don't have to teach me—" Matt quipped. "I already know how to!" He strutted around, fluffing his prickly-pear hair. "'Ooooh, I'm Lizzie,'" Matt cooed, batting his eyes. "'Notice me, Ethan! Notice me, Ethan. Ethan, Ethan, Ethan!'"

Lizzie swung at him, and Matt took off, up the stairs. She raced after him, shrieking. No jury would convict me! Lizzie thought as she pounded up the stairs. Everyone would understand!

Mr. and Mrs. McGuire stared after their children for a moment. Finally, Mrs. McGuire turned to her husband and asked the question that was on both of their minds: "Potatoes or stuffing?"

"My pimple-head brother actually eaves-dropped on us talking about Ethan Craft," Lizzie griped to Miranda as the two headed down the hall toward their first class.

"You should lock him in the basement until he goes away to college," Miranda suggested.

Not a bad idea, Lizzie thought, although she was pretty sure it wouldn't work. "He'll just ooze out through the pipes," Lizzie pointed out, then planted her hands on her hips, exasperated. "He made me sound like such a geek. Like every time I'm around Ethan, I turn into some, like, mindless zombie."

At that moment, His Royal Hotness himself—Ethan Craft—appeared at the end of the hall. He reached the door to the classroom and stopped right in front of Miranda and Lizzie, flashing that megawatt smile. "Hey, Miranda," he said smoothly.

Lizzie's mouth fell open as she gaped at Ethan. Her mind turned slowly, like a gyroscope in Jell-O. His hotness is melting my brain! Lizzie thought.

"Hey, Ethan," Miranda said, like it was no big deal.

"Lizzie," Ethan said, nodding Lizzie's way. "S'up?"

Ethan . . . Speak . . . Me . . . Lizzie thought. Must . . . say . . . words . . . "Oh," Lizzie finally managed to say. "I . . ." What . . . next . . . ?

Say "Hi!" it's not that hard! "How ya' doin', Ethan?" "Good morning," "Yo, dawg, what's crackulatin'?"

Lizzie straightened up and managed a cheery smile. "Hi, Ethan," she said brightly. "Great shirt."

Too bad Ethan had already headed into class. Along with everyone else in the hall.

 Okay. Good start. Next time, just say it while he's still here.

CHAPTER TWO

Mr. Escobar stood at the front of his social studies class, with that smile he always wore before he announced some kind of weird extra-credit assignment.

"You know, kids, the other day I was feeling sorry for myself because I had no shoes," he said slowly, "then I met a man who had no feet."

Lizzie's mouth dropped open in shock. "He had no feet?" she cried, horrified. "How did that happen?"

"Was it a shark attack?" Gordo demanded. He knew all sorts of weird and horrifying facts about sharks, which made going to the beach with him an extremely not-fun experience. "I bet it was a shark attack."

"Well, where did you meet him?" Miranda wanted to know. "Was it in a hospital? Is he okay?"

Mr. Escobar stared at them and shook his head in disbelief. "I didn't *really* meet a man with no feet."

"Then why did you tell us that horrible story?" Miranda demanded. "I'm gonna have nightmares!"

"Yo, Miranda, don't sweat it," Ethan said smoothly. "It just means that there are people who don't have it as good as us."

Miranda stared at him a moment, then nodded. "Oh."

Out of the mouths of babes . . . Lizzie

thought, staring at Ethan in admiration. Or at least one total babe in particular.

Cute and smart. Like Albert Einstein, only without the Three Stooges hair.

Mr. Escobar looked at Ethan, surprised. "Strangely enough, Ethan seems to have grasped the point," the teacher said.

The class cracked up.

"And we should help those less fortunate," Mr. Escobar went on. "That's why I want you to be aware of this Saturday's charity drive." He started handing out a stack of flyers. "And the proceeds are going to go to those less fortunate."

Lizzie looked down at the flyer.

"Asking for donations of canned goods, clothes, and shoes," Miranda read aloud. "Oh, so these kids have feet," she said, clearly relieved. "Good."

"There's a mini-golf tournament," Gordo pointed out. "I could be the announcer. Great, I get extra credit. I unload a ton of canned whitefish—it's like winning the lottery," he said grinning down at the flyer like it was his prize ticket.

Lizzie leaned over to Miranda and whispered, "I just don't think I can do this. I mean, I'm already buried under homework—" Thanks to the mini-magician and his mighty mouth, Lizzie thought, remembering the previous night's debacle. "I need Saturday to get caught up."

"Yo, Mr. Escobar," Ethan called out, raising his hand, "count me in for the tournament."

As though it had a will of its own, Lizzie's hand shot into the air. "I can do this!" she shouted.

And i can impress Ethan!

"I can come early," Lizzie said. Once again, her mouth was running away without her brain.

And i can be with Ethan!

"And bake a few dozen cookies," Lizzie added.

Mr. Escobar smiled and jotted Lizzie's name down on his clipboard.

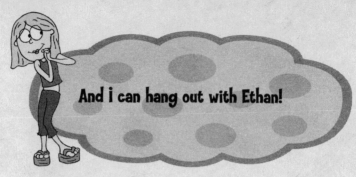

And i can hang out with Ethan!

At that moment, something amazing happened. The stars aligned. The heavens parted. The angels sang. And Ethan Craft leaned toward Lizzie and said, "Lizzie. Helping out. I admire your commitment."

Lizzie's jaw dropped open again. Must . . . Speak . . . Now . . . she thought, floundering in Zombieville. "Thuh-thuh-thuh," Lizzie said.

i just have to be able to talk to Ethan.

"Thuh . . ." Lizzie repeated.

Ethan gave her a weird look and sat back in his chair.

Lizzie sighed. Well, look on the bright side, she told herself. At least you said *something*!

The next morning, Lizzie got up early to pore over cookbooks. She really wanted to impress Ethan with her cooking skills. Lizzie flipped a page. This recipe looked good. She ran her finger down the list of ingredients.

"Mom," Lizzie said as she frowned at the cookbook, "do we have almond paste and raspberries so I can make marzipan meringue with a fruit ganache?"

Mrs. McGuire didn't even bother looking up from the pile of clothes she was folding. "Uh-uh."

"Well, what do we have?" Lizzie huffed, slamming the book onto the countertop. "This is supposed to be a kitchen."

"We have chocolate chips," Lizzie's mom volunteered.

Lizzie thought for a moment. "That'll do." After all, everyone loves chocolate chip cookies, right? Plus, they're hard to mess up.

Mr. McGuire walked into the kitchen with his coffee mug in hand. He was obviously gunning for a refill, but he interrupted his beeline for the coffeepot to frown at the clothes his wife was folding. "What are you doing with my jersey?" he asked.

"I'm taking it to that charity thing," Mrs. McGuire said.

That charity thing? Lizzie thought, horrified. Is my mother actually referring to the upcoming Ethanstravaganza—the most important day of my life—as 'that charity thing'?

Lizzie's dad was completely tuned out to her horror, as usual. "Don't you know what that jersey is?" Mr. McGuire demanded, pointing to the shirt. "The Drive?" he prompted, as though shocked that his wife could have forgotten the importance of this piece of living history that resided in their home. "John Elway marched his team ninety-eight yards in two minutes to tie the game, which he went on to win! I was wearing this while I watched it."

"I didn't know it was so special," Mrs. McGuire said.

"Duh, look, see that?" Mr. McGuire snatched the jersey and pointed to a particularly gross-looking stain. "That's the stain from my cousin Ree-Ree where he high-fived me with a Philly cheesesteak."

Lizzie rolled her eyes. I'm starting to see where Matt gets his weirdness, Lizzie thought.

As though her mind had physically conjured him up, Matt chose that moment to walk into the kitchen carrying rope and a large brass ring. He was wearing a wizard's cap. Can't we send him to wizard school? Lizzie wondered. At least then he'd be out of the way. And maybe he'd be eaten by a stray dragon, or locked up in a dungeon somewhere.

"Hey, Lizzie," Matt said brightly. "I learned a great new trick. Take both ends of the rope."

Lizzie narrowed her eyes at him. "I don't want the rope."

"Take the rope!" Matt insisted.

"I don't want the rope!" Lizzie said. There is no way I'm taking it now, she thought. I don't care if he screams his head off.

"TAKE THE ROPE!" Matt screeched.

"I DON'T WANT THE ROPE!" Lizzie shouted.

Matt glared at her. "TAKE-THE-ROPE!"

"I-DON'T-WANT-THE-ROPE! NOW GET LOST!!!"

"Guys!" Mrs. McGuire said tiredly. "Lizzie,

please don't yell at your brother—" she said in her I'm-running-out-of-patience voice. "And Matt, you cannot make your sister do tricks with you."

"Yes, I can—" Matt insisted. He slapped a handcuff on Lizzie's wrist. The other end was locked around his own wrist. "Okay, for my next illusion, I need a volunteer." He turned to Lizzie. "Oh! How about you, miss?"

"Oh, sure, I volunteer," Lizzie said, grabbing a meat tenderizer off of the counter. "You let me go, and I volunteer not to pound you into stew beef."

Matt's eyebrows flew up, and he stared at the mallet. "Sounds fair!" he said quickly.

At least he's got *some* sense, Lizzie thought.

Matt stared down at the handcuffs. "Abracadabra!" he said, giving the cuffs a yank. They didn't come off. Matt frowned. "It didn't work."

Lizzie rolled her eyes. "Then get the key."

"Oh. The key," Matt said. "Right." He patted his pockets. "Where's the key?"

Lizzie glowered at him. "What?" she asked in a poisonous voice.

Matt gaped at the meat mallet. "Don't make me stew beef!" he begged. "I'm sure I can find it."

Lizzie struggled with the handcuffs, yanking Matt halfway around the kitchen. "Where did you leave it?" she screeched.

Mrs. McGuire looked around, and quickly spotted the key on her desk. She pressed her lips together and looked at her husband, who caught her meaning. Neither one of them said a word.

Meanwhile, Lizzie was yanking like crazy.

"Maybe . . ." Matt said as he was jerked around the kitchen, "it's . . . on . . . the . . . stairs."

"Then go get it," Lizzie said through clenched teeth.

Lizzie headed for the stairs, dragging Matt behind her.

Once the kids were out of the kitchen, Mrs. McGuire hurried to her desk and slipped the key to the handcuffs into her pocket.

"Where else could it be?" Lizzie demanded as she dragged Matt back into the kitchen.

"Don't worry—" Matt said nervously. "We'll find it. Spread out."

The two of them headed off in opposite directions, then found themselves yanked back together by the handcuffs.

"So," Mr. McGuire whispered to his wife, "when are you planning to tell them about the key?"

Mrs. McGuire shrugged. "I think they should stay handcuffed together. They will learn they have to stop bickering and get along with each other, or they'll eat each other alive."

Mr. McGuire nodded. "Either way, we win," he pointed out, taking his jersey from the kitchen.

CHAPTER THREE

Okay, we have to be organized, Lizzie thought as she dragged Matt upstairs. If I were a dumb, moronic, annoying, pinecone-headed little brother, where would I leave a handcuff key?

Probably in the grossest place ever, Lizzie thought.

Sure enough, Matt suggested picking through his dirty clothes to see if the key was in a pocket. Lizzie held her breath, but it wasn't much use. The smell seemed to sink into her skin. And to make matters worse, the key wasn't even in there.

Next, Lizzie tried reaching up on some of the higher shelves, which wasn't so easy with Matt hanging from her arm. Not that the key was there, either.

Okay, okay, *think*, Lizzie commanded herself. Matt spends a lot of time on the couch, playing video games. They headed into the living room, and Lizzie peeked behind the couch while Matt investigated behind the cushions. No luck, although they did get into a pretty rough pillow fight.

Matt thought of looking through his bag of tricks. Lizzie nearly tore it apart, but the key didn't turn up.

What are we going to do? Lizzie thought, beginning to feel desperate. I can't spend the rest of my life chained to the world's freakiest sibling. This has to get solved—right away!

Lizzie raced back into the kitchen and laid out the situation for her parents.

"Now, come on, calm down," Mrs. McGuire said. "Your dad is going to the magic store to get a duplicate key."

"Back in a flash," Mr. McGuire promised.

"He'll get back," Mrs. McGuire said patiently, "you'll get free."

Lizzie glared at her little brother. And not a moment too soon, Lizzie thought.

Mr. McGuire was back in less than twenty minutes. "I'm back," he singsonged cheerfully.

"Oh, yes!" Lizzie said. "We're free."

Mr. McGuire grimaced. "Not exactly," he admitted.

"Dad, the key?" Matt said, his voice rising in panic. "Where's the key?"

"The key," Mr. McGuire said, heaving a deep breath. "Here's the thing about the key. There is no key."

"What?" Lizzie cried.

"Well, the magic shop was closed," Mr. McGuire explained. "It's a magician's holiday. Who knew?" He shrugged.

See? Send an amateur to shop, and that's what you get. Nothin'.

"But the good news is, there's a joke shop over in Stanton," Mr. McGuire said quickly, "and I'm sure they've got a ton of 'em."

"Dad," Lizzie said gesturing wildly, and yanking Matt around with every move, "I've got to be at the charity event in, like, two hours!"

"Don't worry—it's not that far," Mr. McGuire said smoothly. "I'll be back in plenty of time for Mom to make it to your thing. Without Matt."

Lizzie glared at Matt. I'm not going with him, even if I have to cut off my arm, Lizzie thought. No wait, scratch that. Even if I have to cut off *Matt's* arm.

"Hey, don't look at me," Matt said with a sneer. "I'd rather chew my hand off than spend the rest of the day with you."

Lizzie narrowed her eyes at him. Careful, little brother, she thought. You might just get your wish.

Lizzie and Mrs. McGuire walked through the entrance to the mini-golf course, waving to people they knew. Lizzie couldn't believe what a huge success this fund-raiser seemed to be— the place was packed with kids and charity booths for clothes, toys, books, canned food—everything!

"Lizzie, there you are," Miranda said as she rushed over to join them. "Hey, hey, finally. Ethan's been asking about you," she added, waggling her eyebrows. Miranda pointed across the mini-golf course, where Ethan was practicing his putts. Just then, Ethan looked up. Spotting Lizzie, he gave her a friendly wave.

Lizzie's stomach flipped as she waved back.

"Okay, honey," Mrs. McGuire said, "I'm going to check in over at the clothing donation table. Have a good time."

Oh, no, Lizzie thought as her mother started to step away. I never thought that I would stoop to this, but please don't leave me, Mom!

"Bye, Mom!" Matt shouted. The handcuffs jingled a little as he waved to Mrs. McGuire.

Miranda gaped at Matt. "Lizzie, there's a little kid on your arm."

"Oh, you noticed," Lizzie said, her voice dripping with sarcasm. She glared at Matt and told him, "Start chewing."

"Spare change for the needy kids?" Miranda asked a passerby hopefully as she held out a tin can. She had a soda in the other hand. A guy dropped a dollar into the can and walked off. "Oh, thank you, sir," Miranda called after him gratefully. "Mad props on that one."

Miranda walked over to Lizzie and handed her the soda.

Lizzie took it, miserably, as she leaned against a photo booth. She and Matt were in the arcade, and Lizzie was trying to stand so that her handcuffs weren't noticeable. But it wasn't working very well.

"Hey," Miranda said. "So, how are you going to make this work?" she added, nodding at the handcuffs.

"Simple," Lizzie replied. "I'm going to wait here until my dad comes with the extra key."

"Well, what if you see someone you know?" Miranda asked.

"Plan B," Lizzie explained, demonstrating.

"Waagh!" Matt shouted as Lizzie swung her handcuffed arm, shoving Matt into the photo booth. Pay no attention to that boy behind the curtain, Lizzie thought.

"Lizzie, listen—Plan B!" Miranda whispered desperately. "Plan B!"

Oh, no. Why *now?* she thought as she saw Ethan approaching. Any other moment of any other day, Lizzie thought desperately as she moved in front of the photo booth, making sure Matt was hidden.

"Lizzie," Ethan said smoothly. "Glad you could make it."

"Hi, Ethan!" Lizzie said nervously. "How's the . . . putting?"

"I start in a couple of minutes," Ethan replied. He held out a large carton of popcorn. "You want some popcorn?"

"Oh, no thanks," Lizzie said quickly. "I had a really big lunch."

Ethan turned to Miranda. "You want some?"

Just then, Matt's hand snaked out from behind the curtain, emerging from under Lizzie's armpit so that it looked like her own! Lizzie stared at it, horrified. What the heck is that maniac doing? she thought as Matt grabbed an enormous fistful of popcorn and crammed it into Lizzie's mouth. Lizzie had no choice but to chew like a maniac.

Ethan frowned in confusion. "Take all you want," he offered as "Lizzie's hand" reached for more. "I have plenty."

Miranda stared at the scene in horror as Matt's hand shoved more popcorn into

Lizzie's mouth. She couldn't chew fast enough. Lizzie ducked away and took a long sip of soda as Matt's hand, reloaded with popcorn, flailed about in search of her mouth.

"She really loves popcorn," Miranda said quickly, covering for Lizzie. "But she's allergic, so she can't have any." Miranda grabbed Matt's hand and pinned it against the side of the booth.

"Ooof!" Matt said.

"Ooof!" Lizzie repeated, trying to make it seem as though Matt's voice were her own. "Good popcorn. Popcorn . . ." Lizzie said with her mouth full.

Mr. Escobar picked that moment to walk over and join them.

"Ethan," Mr. Escobar said, slapping Ethan on the shoulder, "in the tournament, *bon chance*. That's French for . . ." Noticing Ethan's blank stare, Mr. Escobar shook his head. "Oh, never mind. Miranda, Lizzie, could you give me a hand hanging a banner?"

"I'm really sorry," Lizzie said sincerely. She was still trying to chew. "I'm really busy now."

Mr. Escobar heaved a heavy sigh and peered at her over the tops of his blue-tinted specs. "Lizzie, I find it very vexing that you don't show more initiative."

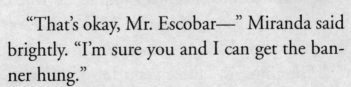

i'd like to see you show initiative while you're handcuffed to your little brother!

"That's okay, Mr. Escobar—" Miranda said brightly. "I'm sure you and I can get the banner hung."

Mr. Escobar grinned. "Attagirl."

"Good luck," Miranda whispered to Lizzie as she walked off with Mr. Escobar.

"So . . ." Lizzie said as a flash went off from within the photo booth. "Do you think you'll win the tournament?"

"I hope so," Ethan said warmly. "I love helping kids out."

Oh, no, Lizzie thought as she spotted Matt's hand wriggling out underneath her armpit again. He reached up and started treating her face like Silly Putty, contorting her face with his hand. The worst part was, it looked like she was doing it to herself! So, without any other option, she smiled, as though making herself look as if she had a pig nose was the most normal thing to do when one was chatting with the High King of Hotness himself.

"The thing is," Ethan said, obviously trying to ignore Lizzie's freakish behavior, "my dad was out of work for a couple years when I was little, so I really know what it's like to not have a lot."

"Mmm, hmm." Lizzie did her best to sound sympathetic as she racked her brain to think of new ways that she could torture Matt once they got home.

Ethan frowned as Matt's hand grabbed Lizzie's chin and started shaking her head backward and forward. "Are you okay?" he asked.

"Oh," Lizzie said as she dumped her soda into the photo booth. Finally, she had a free hand. Matt let out a yelp as she grabbed his hand. "Just fine." She wrestled with Matt's hand, trying to pin it down. "Just a little nervous from all the excitement. I think I better stay in here for a little while, then I'll come out and watch you golf. Okay?"

"Yeah . . . okay," Ethan said slowly. "See you there."

Just as Ethan turned to leave, Kate flounced over. "Ethan!" she chirped. "I brought you a bottle of water in case it gets hot outside."

Lizzie rolled her eyes. Great, she thought. Now Kate looks sensitive and thoughtful, and I look completely nuts.

"Thanks," Ethan told Kate warmly. "I've got some mean competition out there."

Kate batted her eyelashes at him. "Do you mind if I watch?"

Grrr, Lizzie thought, frustrated. Look at her—flirting with Ethan like she doesn't have a brain in her head. It's so unfair—that should be *me*!

"No problem." Ethan held out his arm, and Kate linked hers through his. Then they walked off together.

Lizzie glared after them as Matt fished around the slot in the photo booth and pulled out a bunch of pictures printed on stickers.

"Cool," Matt said as he held up the photos. "Pictures."

Lizzie scowled at him and stuck one of the photo stickers to his forehead. "Come on."

"Oh, thank you," Mrs. McGuire said as she took a bag of clothes from a donor. "Every bit helps." Mrs. McGuire reached into the bag as the woman walked off. "Who wears *these*?" she asked out loud as she held up a pair of pants big enough to use as a camping tent.

But that wasn't the biggest mystery of the day. Of course, the bigger question was how long could Lizzie and Matt stand being hand-cuffed together before one of them snapped? Mrs. McGuire pulled out her cell phone. It was time to check in with Home Base.

"Hello?" Mr. McGuire said on the second ring.

"Hey, honey," Mrs. McGuire said. "We're here."

"Hi," Mr. McGuire said with a small chuckle. "When would you like me to 'find the key'?"

"Oh, I'd give it a couple of hours," Mrs. McGuire said. "You've got a free day at home."

Mr. McGuire pumped his fist in silent joy. Now he had all day to watch football and eat cheesy corn chips—yes! But he knew he'd better not act too happy about it, or his wife might suspect that he wasn't going to spend his time productively, cleaning out the gutters and whatnot. "Well, whatever," Mr. McGuire said casually. "So, how're they doing?"

Mrs. McGuire looked over to where Lizzie and Matt were standing. Matt was wearing a virtual reality helmet, trying to play a video game. And he was yanking Lizzie around like mad while he played.

"Matt!" Lizzie snapped in a venomous voice.

"I'd say they still have some things to work out," Mrs. McGuire said into the phone calmly. Then she said good-bye and hung up. She knew it wasn't very nice, but the truth was that a small part of Mrs. McGuire was enjoying watching her children drive each other crazy. It had to teach them *something*.

"You should see me on the *Cyborg Battalion*," Matt said eagerly as he dragged a bored-looking Lizzie toward another video game. "I own that game."

Suddenly, a tough-looking kid about Matt's age stepped up to *Cyborg Battalion*.

"Actually," Matt said quickly as he spotted the kid, "I don't want to play. I don't like that kid."

Lizzie frowned. It wasn't like Matt to back off so easily. "Why, what's wrong with him?" she asked. She peered over at the tough kid. He looked kind of like a bully.

Matt pressed his lips together as he watched Heywood Briggs take control of the video game. Basically, when it came to school-yard torture, Heywood was a genius—every morning he would shove Matt up against a locker and demand his lunch money, or else he would put Matt into a headlock, or kneel on Matt's chest, or steal Matt's baseball cap and play keep-away with it, or pull Matt's shirt up over his head, then knock him down. But there was no way Matt was going to tell Lizzie the truth—that Heywood Briggs beat up on Matt even more than she did herself! Instead, Matt said, "Nothing, he's always telling stupid jokes, and I get tired pretending to laugh. C'mon," Matt said, yanking on the handcuffs, "let's go watch the golf."

"No!" Lizzie wailed. "I can't. I just told Ethan that I have to stay in here for a while. If I go out there, he'll think I'm a complete baboon."

"Trust me—" Matt said seriously, "there's a million other reasons for him to think you're a complete baboon."

No thanks to you and your popcorn antics, Lizzie thought. But she had to admit that Matt had a point, so she followed him out of the arcade.

CHAPTER FOUR

The doorbell rang and Mr. McGuire hurried to answer it—sliding down the banister.

"Keep the change," Mr. McGuire said as the delivery guy handed over a pizza, a bucket of chicken wings, a six-pack of soda, and an enormous bag of potato chips. Mr. McGuire was wearing his Lucky Football Jersey—he had a feeling that this was going to be one of the greatest days of his life.

"Yeah!" Mr. McGuire said as he headed over to the couch. "Here we go, football, here we go, football!" he chanted, cranking up the volume on the TV set. He settled onto the sofa and cracked open a soda. Mr. McGuire lay back, getting even more comfortable.

He took a bite of pizza and sank deeper into the couch. He was really, really comfortable.

Maybe a little too comfortable.

In thirty seconds, Mr. McGuire was fast asleep.

"Ethan Craft lines up his putt on the par four third," Gordo said in a hushed tone as his voice was broadcast over the speaker system. "It's a seventeen-yard dogleg left with some serious trouble in the form of a bendy horseshoe shape." Gordo looked down at the index cards he was given that had advertisements for some of the booths scrawled on them. He began to read.

"Say," Gordo announced, giving it his best gooey announcer's voice, "now's a great time to enjoy an ice-cold cherry slush or zesty, south-of-the-border nachos. *Cinco de* my-oh-my, they're good. Real cheese, fifty cents extra."

Lizzie applauded politely along with the rest of the crowd, as Ethan sank his putt. Ethan looked up and, spotting Lizzie, gave her a friendly wave. But Lizzie quickly put her right hand down. She didn't want Ethan to see that she was handcuffed to her gross little brother. She waved back with her other hand.

Just then, a little piece of ice dinged Matt in the forehead. Matt turned and saw Heywood, who grinned and hurled a slice of pickle in Matt's direction.

Lizzie frowned. "Matt, why is that bad-joke kid throwing food at you?" she asked. "What did you do to him?"

Whatever was going on, Lizzie knew that she didn't want to be a part of it. All she needed was pickle juice on her shirt! Then Ethan will think I'm nuts *and* a slob, she thought.

"I didn't do anything to him," Matt said miserably.

"Oh, so he's just doing it 'cause he feels like it," Lizzie said, her voice dripping sarcasm. "Picking on you for no reason."

Lizzie waited a moment for Matt to say something sarcastic back, or to admit that he had flushed the bad-joke kid's joke book down the toilet, or something, but Matt didn't reply. He just stood there, frowning at the bad-joke kid. The tough, mean-looking, five-times-the-size-of-Matt-bad-joke kid. . . .

"Omigosh," Lizzie said quickly, realizing the truth. "He really *does* pick on you?"

"Yeah," Matt said in a sullen voice. "So?"

"So, nothing," Lizzie replied. "I just couldn't think of any reason why anyone would want to pick on a great kid like you," she added in an innocent voice. "Oh," she said, pretending that the reason had just occurred to her, "maybe it's because you go around handcuffing people." She gave her arm a yank. "Come on, let's go to the next hole."

Lizzie dragged Matt away, just as Miranda trotted past. She was hounding a kid in a pink shirt who was clearly trying to escape from her. "Maybe you don't hear so good," Miranda said, shaking her donation can. "Charity. You know what that means?" she asked sarcastically. "Hey, don't be walkin' away from me!"

Lizzie dragged Matt around the mini-golf course to watch each one of Ethan's attempts. Next up was The Windmill. Then the Psycho house. Then a bridge over a lake.

"Man, this is dull," Gordo said to himself as he watched Ethan prepare his putt. Again. "Ethan Craft draws back his flat-stick and rolls his rock," Gordo said into the microphone. He had a sneaking suspicion that some of these spectators weren't even really listening to his commentary. "It's on line, but––but what's this? King Tut's mummy has suddenly come alive and is stalking the gallery, tearing the heads off innocent spectators!"

Everyone ignored Gordo as Ethan sank the putt.

"And now the Mir Space Station is falling out of the sky!" Gordo announced. "Oh, the humanity! Mercy, a piece of debris is heading right at me, and I . . . Ugh . . ." Gordo hissed into the microphone, making static noises, then unplugged the mike and set it down. "I'm gonna go get me some nachos."

Lizzie started to drag Matt toward the next hole. But before they had gone two steps, Heywood snuck up behind Matt and tripped him. Lizzie fell over, too.

"Have a nice trip," Heywood said with a sneer. His eyes fell on the handcuffs. "I see you girls stick together."

Lizzie whirled, glaring at Heywood dangerously. "I am *not* in the mood!" she snapped as she stood up. "I've got a teacher who thinks I'm lazy, I've got Kate Sanders sniffing around a guy I like, I've got a stress pimple on my neck the size of a hockey puck, and I've got seventy pounds of useless fat chained to my wrist. So unless you want me to force-feed you a set of golf clubs, I suggest you get out of my face, and I mean *now*, you rat-head, weasel-eyed punk!"

Heywood ducked away from Lizzie, then ran off.

Lizzie looked down at Matt. "Come on!" she barked.

Matt smiled at her. "Thanks."

Lizzie snorted impatiently. "I didn't do it for you," she said. "I did it because no one gets to beat up on you but me."

"Well, it was still kind of nice," Matt said, "in a twisted kind of way."

"Well," Lizzie said grudgingly, "I didn't need one more thing messing up my day."

"I guess you do kind of have a lot of things going on," Matt said apologetically.

Lizzie sighed. "Tell me about it."

"I didn't think it'd be so difficult being a teenager," Matt said.

Lizzie snorted. "Just wait until you find out about peer pressure and hygiene products and when Mom starts having 'important talks' with you."

Matt thought for a moment, then shuddered.

It was all much, much worse than he had ever imagined. "Sorry about the handcuffs thing," Matt said sincerely. "But if I had to spend the day with a dopey sister, I'm glad it was you."

Lizzie laughed softly. "Thanks. If I had to spend the day with a dorkhead brother, you probably weren't the worst one," she admitted.

Matt shrugged.

Kate picked that moment to flounce over. "Hi, Lizzie," Kate said, giving Lizzie a little wave. "It's true—" Kate said, eyeing the handcuffs, "you are wearing your brother as a charm bracelet. Interesting fashion choice. You know, you missed Ethan's hole-in-one." Kate flashed Lizzie an evil smile. "Luckily, I was there to cheer for him. I've got to get back there—he relies on my support." Kate strutted away.

Lizzie wished that she could think of a

snappy comeback, but it was hard to save face while chained to someone who's in elementary school. Why even bother? she wondered.

Matt watched Kate walk away. "I don't like her," he said, wrinkling his nose.

"Me, neither," Lizzie agreed.

Matt thought for a moment. "I've got an idea."

Lizzie and Matt hurried after Kate. "Hey, Kate—" Matt said, holding out a small tin can. "Want a macadamia nut?"

Kate looked doubtful. "Uh . . ."

"They're from Hawaii," Matt singsonged, goading her. "And Ethan *loves* them."

"Okay. Gimmee those." Kate grabbed the can and twisted it open. The minute the top came off, three-foot-long spring snakes flew out. Kate cried out in surprise, then took a startled step backward, falling into a water hazard.

Finally. There's a reason for Matt's existence.

"Oh, come on," Lizzie said to Matt as Kate floundered around in the water, "let's get out of here."

"Hey—kids!" shouted a voice.

Lizzie and Matt stopped in their tracks. We're so very busted, Lizzie thought. She and Matt turned to see who had caught them. Just one more thing to top off this already-perfect day, Lizzie thought sarcastically.

She and Matt turned to see their dad—he was on the other side of the water hazard. He hadn't seen them trick Kate, after all. "I got the key," Mr. McGuire called, tossing it to them. He chucked it all the way across the water.

Lizzie caught the key in her cuffed hand.

Is this really happening? Lizzie thought as she unlocked the cuffs. Is something actually going right? The handcuffs sprang open. "Yes!" Lizzie hissed, throwing her hands in the air.

Then, something amazing happened. She actually gave Matt a high-five.

"So, how'd the clothing drive go?" Lizzie asked her mom later that day.

"Oh, it went well," Mrs. McGuire said. "And if there are any kids who weigh four hundred pounds and are needy, they'll be extremely well-dressed."

"Yo, Lizzie," Ethan said as he walked up to her.

Lizzie smiled. "Hi, Ethan."

"That's Ethan Craft?" Mr. McGuire whispered to his wife.

Mrs. McGuire nodded. "Yeah."

Lizzie's parents stepped toward the arcade, so that Lizzie could chat with Ethan in private.

"So, I heard you won," Lizzie said to Ethan. "That's great."

"Thanks," Ethan said with a grin. "I heard you spent the whole day with your cool little brother. I *love* that little guy." Ethan laughed and shook his head. "Listen, a whole bunch of us are going out for pizza. You wanna come?"

Just as Lizzie opened her mouth to say yes, she heard a yelp. Over Ethan's shoulder, she spotted Matt on the other side of a table from Heywood. Actually, it looked like Matt was trying to use the table to block Heywood. Matt darted to the right, and Heywood darted after him. Lizzie narrowed her eyes. Oh, no he didn't, Lizzie thought.

"Lizzie . . . ?" Ethan prompted.

Lizzie gazed up into Ethan's gorgeous eyes, then peered over at Matt. It looked like her little brother was definitely headed for a good pounding from that bully. *That should make me happy . . . Lizzie realized . . . but for some reason, it doesn't.* "You know what?" Lizzie said suddenly. "You guys go ahead. I've got a needy little kid I've gotta take care of." She darted after Matt, screeching, "Heywood! You're roadkill!"

Hey, Lizzie thought as she raced after Heywood. *Who says I can't do a good deed now and then? Even for my porcupine-headed little brother . . . who really isn't* that *bad, after all.*

Lizzie McGuire

PART TWO

CHAPTER ONE

Lizzie McGuire squinted in the sunlight that streamed into the courtyard as she looked up at Ms. Dew, who was hobbling toward the podium. Ms. Dew, Lizzie's art teacher had taken a semester off for "personal reasons." Everyone had his or her own idea as to what the "personal reason" really was. Lizzie glanced over at her best friends, Miranda Sanchez and David "Gordo" Gordon. Miranda had guessed that Ms. Dew was vacationing in Morocco, but Gordo thought that she had gone off on a retreat with Tibetan monks.

Wherever she went, Lizzie thought, it couldn't have been too great. After all, she was right back here, standing at a podium at Hillridge Junior High.

"I can't believe Ms. Dew is back," Gordo whispered to Miranda.

"I think the semester break did her some good," Lizzie said brightly. "I mean, she looks a lot less nervous."

"Go Ms. Dew!" Miranda shouted out.

Ms. Dew flinched at Miranda's outburst and looked like she was ready to bolt.

Well, maybe a *little* less nervous, Lizzie revised mentally.

"I think maybe we should keep our voices down," Gordo suggested in a low voice, "and not make any sudden movements."

"Good afternoon, students," Ms. Dew said

in her quavering voice. Lizzie glanced at the art teacher's knuckles, which were white as she gripped the podium for dear life. "I just wanted to say that it's so nice to be back. And while I was away I really missed the school. So, I thought that my first art project back should be about school unity."

School unity—cool idea, Lizzie thought. She looked around at the crowd of kids and locked eyes with Kate Sanders, the most snob-iferous queen bee at school. Kate gave Lizzie a sneer, then turned back to face Ms. Dew.

i'm all for school unity as long as it doesn't involve Kate.

"So this Friday we are all going to put our painted handprints on the courtyard wall for a Mural of Togetherness," Ms. Dew explained. She held up her hands and mimed pressing them against a wall.

I guess she thinks we'll need a little help with such a complicated assignment, Lizzie thought.

"So, please, make sure you don't leave your hands at home!" Ms. Dew laced her fingers together, pleading.

Lizzie stared at her friends. Don't leave our hands at home? Lizzie wondered. Is this a common problem? I'm starting to think that Ms. Dew really has kind of lost it.

Ms. Dew's face fell. "That was a joke."

"Ha-ha-ha-ha!" Miranda let out a belly laugh that echoed through the courtyard.

"Miranda!" Lizzie whispered fiercely as Ms. Dew started at Miranda's laugh.

"What?" Miranda demanded. "I'm just trying to be supportive." She shrugged. "Plus, it sounds like a pretty cool project."

Gordo snorted. "It sounds to me like the school's trying to save money on repainting the courtyard by getting us to do it."

Lizzie rolled her eyes. Gordo could be so cynical. The school was always coming up with cool projects for the students . . .

School painting project, school car wash project, school clean-up project . . . Hey, wait, maybe Gordo's right!

That's the thing about Gordo, Lizzie thought as she grinned at her friend. He may be cynical, but he's usually got a point.

"So," Lizzie said to her mother as she carried her cereal bowl to the breakfast table the next morning, "I was trying to figure out what color we should do our handprints for the school mural of unity." Of course, the "we" she was talking about was she, Gordo and Miranda. They had agreed to use three different colors, but to put their handprints on the wall together.

"Oh, that's so funny," Mrs. McGuire said brightly, as she struggled to open a stubborn jar lid, "because I just read this great article about how the color of your front door should reflect the personalities of the people who live in the house."

Mrs. McGuire blinked innocently at Lizzie over the tops of her rectangular glasses.

Oh, no she doesn't. I'm painting the school for free. Mom's not roping me into doing the front door, too.

"That's pretty cool," Lizzie said casually. If she asks me to help paint the door, I'll just tell her that I have to go to the library—for the rest of my life, she thought.

"Yeah," Mrs. McGuire agreed, "so today, I'm painting our door red." Mrs. McGuire struggled with the jar of all-natural peanut butter, but the lid still wouldn't budge.

"Red?" Lizzie frowned. "What's wrong with white, like we have now?" Lizzie liked the white door—it was basic. And it coordinates with everything, Lizzie added mentally.

"Well, red's exciting," Mrs. McGuire explained, "and we're the exciting McGuires."

Lizzie raised her eyebrows and gave her mother a dubious look. The exciting McGuires? Lizzie's mother was the kind of person who got a thrill when twenty-packs of toilet paper went on sale. It was hardly like their house was adventure-central. "Oh," Lizzie said, as she gestured for her mom to hand over the jar.

Mrs. McGuire seemed to get the hint. "Okay," she said slowly, "I can look at some other colors. Thank you," Mrs. McGuire added as Lizzie opened the jar she had been struggling with with a single twist.

Just then, Lizzie's little brother Matt walked—or rather, squished—into the kitchen. His slippers were soaking wet!

"I think I've got a problem," Matt said.

"Yeah," Lizzie snapped, "I think it's wetting the bed."

Mrs. McGuire gave her daughter a warning glance. "Lizzie," she said, then turned to her son. "What happened, Matt?"

"I don't know," Matt insisted as he pulled off his soggy slippers. "All I did was put on my slippers. And they're soaked." He flapped the slippers back and forth, splattering water everywhere.

Mrs. McGuire shook her head and reached for the slippers. "Oh, no. Stop, stop. Come here." She motioned Matt over to the kitchen island and had him hand her his slippers. Water splashed into the sink as Mrs. McGuire wrung them out.

Lizzie rolled her eyes as she started to mix up the peanut butter. Whatever this slipper problem was about, she was sure she didn't want to be a part of it.

A moment later, Mr. McGuire rushed into the kitchen. "A pipe burst in the wall in Matt's room!" he cried. "The floor is soaked. I had to turn off the water!"

Mrs. McGuire's eyes widened in dismay. "Oh, no," she said with a groan. "We have to move everything out of his room."

Lizzie continued to concentrate on the

peanut butter as her mom raced out of the kitchen to take care of Matt's stuff. Not my room, not my problem, Lizzie thought. True, this wasn't a very nice thought. Then again, Matt wasn't a very nice *person* as far as Lizzie was concerned, and she had no interest in giving him the smallest scrap of sympathy.

"You know what," Mr. McGuire announced, "I'm going to call work and tell them I'm not coming in, because we're going to have to move Matt into Lizzie's room until we can get it fixed."

"What?" Lizzie shrieked. She looked over at Matt, who was busily squeezing out his wet slippers so that the water dripped all over the floor. "No, no, no! Porcupine-head is not sleeping in my bedroom."

"Well, where do you think he's going to sleep?" Mr. McGuire demanded. "Outside?"

Lizzie frowned. Her father could be so

sarcastic. Of *course* she wouldn't make Matt sleep outside—that was ridiculous. Lizzie was thinking he could sleep in the garage. "Actually—"

"Don't!" Mr. McGuire commanded, holding up his hand, traffic-cop style. He shook his head, then walked out of the kitchen.

"Yeah," Matt added with a smug little grin. "Don't."

Lizzie narrowed her eyes at him. "Oh, you!" she growled, then took off after her brother, who ran shrieking from the room.

Hey! i am the child with the most seniority here! i deserve some respect and i deserve it now. . . . Please?

CHAPTER TWO

Lizzie sighed and looked around. Why do we always have to go through these boring fire drills, she wondered. I mean, do we really need all this practice to teach people how to get out of the school? I do it every day at three o'clock.

"Very good fire drill, people," Ms. Dew said in an edgy voice as she buzzed past Lizzie, Miranda, and Gordo. "Now remember, stay quietly in line until the 'all clear' bell. It's just a drill. Don't panic." Ms. Dew repeated, her voice rising, "It's just a drill!"

Gordo shook his head. "I don't think she's gonna make it to Friday."

"I don't think she'll even make it to lunch," Miranda added.

"Oh, come on you guys," Lizzie said suddenly, "everybody is doing the mural, let's go find a place to put our handprints."

"Why do you have to be so cooperative?" Gordo demanded. "Why can't you be bitter and cynical, like a normal student?"

Miranda rolled her eyes at him. "Gordo, it's just a goofy art project," she insisted. "It can't hurt. Plus, we get out of school for half a day."

Gordo shrugged. "Whatever."

Lizzie took that as Gordo's version of school spirit. "Great," Lizzie said. "Let's find a place."

The three friends walked over to the wall, which was already blocked by a crowd of kids.

"How about right there in the middle?"

Gordo asked, pointing to the exact center of the wall.

Lizzie nodded. "Cool," she said, "that's fine with me."

Just then, Kate walked over and gave Lizzie a scornful glance. "Uh, the middle?" she said in her best you-have-got-to-be-joking voice. "I don't think so. The cheerleaders are putting their handprints in the middle, and the jocks are going next to them." Kate gave Lizzie a tight little smile and gestured toward the end of the wall. "Maybe you guys could go by the trash can with the chess club geeks," she suggested, "if they'll let you." She folded her arms across her chest.

Lizzie frowned. "I thought this was supposed to be about unity," she protested. "I thought we were all supposed to blend our handprints in together."

"Uh, yeah," Kate said, flipping her long

honey-colored hair over her shoulder. "You guys go be all unified over there."

"Fine," Lizzie snapped, "we *will* go put our handprints over there."

I don't want to be with stupid old Kate, anyway, Lizzie thought as she looked over toward the geek end of the wall.

"Hey, hey, hey!" Larry Tudgeman—king of the Hillridge geeks—said suddenly, moving to intercept the trio. He put his arms around Lizzie's and Gordo's shoulders and gave Lizzie a knowing grin. "Do you guys know Jar-Jar Binks's middle name?"

Gordo stared at Larry. "Uh, Jar?" he guessed.

Lizzie blinked and nodded. Hey—good guess, she thought, but Larry just ignored Gordo.

"Are you Jedi Knights?" Tudgeman demanded. "Were you born on the planet Alderon?"

Lizzie lifted her eyebrows. "Uh, no."

"No, you weren't," Larry said, pointing toward the end of the wall, "so that quadrant is off-limits to you."

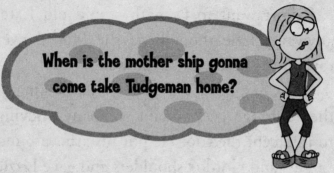

When is the mother ship gonna come take Tudgeman home?

Miranda threw up her hand in disgust. "Okay—news flash, people!" she shouted. "It's just a wall!"

Larry ignored her and started picking his nose.

I hope he washes his hands before he presses them against the wall, Lizzie thought.

"Last week you guys were bouncing a

stupid ball off of it," Miranda went on. "And this week you guys are treating it like it's some new planet."

Seriously, Miranda is right, Lizzie thought. Where's Ms. Dew? Maybe she can talk some sense into these people.

Just then, Ms. Dew ran by. "Don't panic!" she cried. "It's just a drill! Don't panic! Don't panic!"

"I think we're gonna have to do this one for Ms. Dew," Gordo said.

"This is so unfair," Lizzie griped. "There's no room for me on the wall. And there's no room for me at home."

"What do you mean, there's no room for you at home?" Miranda asked Lizzie.

Lizzie bit her lip. She really didn't want to talk about it. On the other hand, she thought, if you can't complain to your best friends, who can you complain to? "Well, my parents want Matt to move into my bedroom," Lizzie confessed.

Miranda made a small choking noise and shook her head. "Oh, that's not gonna happen."

"You mean, 'that's not going to happen *again*,'" Lizzie corrected. "We already tried that when I was, like, five, and even then he was whipping me in the head with his teething ring." Lizzie shuddered at the memory. Matt had really good aim, especially considering that he was a baby back then. It was actually kind of scary.

"Why do you have to share a room with Matt?" Gordo asked. "Are your parents having a baby?"

A chill shivered down Lizzie's spine as the image of having to deal with another "Matt" flashed through her mind. One was enough, thank you very much.

"No!" Lizzie answered with a shudder. "Some kind of pipe busted in Matt's room. So, until it gets repaired, Stinkboy is with me."

The all-clear bell trilled and Lizzie turned to leave. Just then, Ms. Dew came racing into the courtyard, screaming, "It's another fire drill!"

"Uh, Ms. Dew," Gordo said helpfully, touching her shoulder. "Ms. Dew, that was just the all-clear bell."

Ms. Dew took a deep breath and composed herself. "I knew that," she said in a flat voice, then pushed her glasses up higher on her nose and walked off.

Does she realize that she has another pair of glasses on top of her head? Lizzie wondered.

"You're right," Lizzie whispered to Miranda, "she definitely needs us."

CHAPTER THREE

Lizzie frowned at the front door, which her mother was busily painting a bright clover green. I guess Mom finally accepted that we aren't the "exciting McGuires," Lizzie thought, but I wonder what this color means. "So, I guess, we're green with envy?" Lizzie suggested.

Mrs. McGuire stood back and stared at the door. "That's what you get?" she asked. "No, it's supposed to be fresh, like springtime."

Well, I guess Matt is kind of fresh, Lizzie

thought. But Stinkboy sure doesn't smell like springtime. Speak of the devil—literally. At that moment, Matt walked out of his room with a huge box of stuff and headed into Lizzie's room.

"So who let the weasel out of his cage?" Lizzie demanded, glaring at her brother.

"Okay," Lizzie's mom said with a sigh, "Matt and your Dad are just moving a few of Matt's things into your room."

Lizzie's eyes widened. "Matt's stuff?" she snapped. "In *my* room? How will I ever get the stench out?" I have to stop this madness, Lizzie thought as she raced up the stairs. Before my room is infested with bad Mattitude.

Lizzie stopped in her doorway and gaped in horror. It was even worse than she had thought. Lizzie's dad had actually rearranged the furniture so that Matt's bed could fit next to hers. And some of her brother's useless, putrid junk was on her floor!

"Dad!" Lizzie wailed as she watched her father fiddle with the edge of Matt's bed. "What are you doing?"

"Getting Matt's bed set up," Mr. McGuire said, like it was no big deal he was ruining Lizzie's life.

Just then, a tall young guy in carpenter jeans and a T-shirt walked into Lizzie's room. *Oh, please tell me that they're not building any special shelves in here for Matt's junk,* Lizzie begged silently, *or I swear, I think I'll lose it.*

"Oh, hey," Mr. McGuire said to the guy, "you're here to fix the pipe, right? It's the next room. I'll be right there."

The guy nodded and walked out.

Lizzie folded her arms across her chest. She didn't want her dad to get all involved in fixing the pipe, and forget about the essential problem. "Dad, why is Matt's bed in here?" Lizzie demanded.

"What do you expect him to do, Lizzie?" Mr. McGuire asked, shaking his head. "Curl up in a corner?"

Of course not in the corner. There's room in the closet.

Lizzie heaved a deep breath, trying to be patient. "I thought he had a sleeping bag."

"Lizzie, this isn't a camping trip," Mr. McGuire snapped. He gave her a disapproving look, then walked out of the room.

Meanwhile, Matt began to tack a poster to the wall.

Oh, no, Lizzie thought as she took a look at

the poster! My room cannot go from cool to fool in under five seconds!

"Uh, no," Lizzie said. "That does not go on my wall."

"But it's Weird Al!" Matt cried. "He's way cool."

Lizzie cocked an eyebrow. Matt was wearing a fake "arrow through the head" and big-nose-and-glasses disguise. Obviously, the ability to judge what was cool did not run in the family. "Yeah, well, if Weird Al touches my wall, he'll come down as Shredded Al," Lizzie cracked. "Okay? No." She shoved the poster back into Matt's hands.

"You just don't appreciate good music," Matt insisted. But he didn't put up the poster.

Instead, he started pulling more stuff out of a large cardboard box. Lizzie watched in disbelief and horror as he pulled out a rubber snake, a fake human hand, and slime.

"Well, I'd really appreciate it if you kept your infested trash out of my room," Lizzie said.

"Mom said I could bring the stuff that I need into your room," Matt replied.

Lizzie narrowed her eyes.

i know what Matt *needs* . . .
his own room!

Meanwhile, Mr. McGuire was in Matt's room, talking to Wally, the construction guy. Wally had pulled back the carpet in the corner. Sure enough, the floor underneath was soaked.

"So, what do you think?" Mr. McGuire asked nervously.

Wally shrugged. "I think you've got a leak."

"Right," Mr. McGuire said, nodding. "So,

how long do you think it would it take you to fix it?"

"Oh, about an hour or two."

"That's great!" Mr. McGuire said in relief. "So you'll be finished today."

Wally chuckled and shook his head. "That's a good one," he said, slapping Mr. McGuire on the arm. He was still chuckling as he walked out of the room.

"So, uh, by tomorrow it could all be fixed, right?" Mr. McGuire asked hopefully as he squished across Matt's carpet and followed Wally downstairs.

"Well," Wally said slowly, "tomorrow I'll have to buy my materials and hire my crew."

Mr. McGuire grimaced, but he didn't let Wally's answer get him down. Obviously, this was a small problem. It couldn't possibly take *that* long to fix the pipe. "Then how about the next day?"

Wally thought for a moment. "Yeah," he said finally.

Mr. McGuire smiled in relief. Two days. That wouldn't be so bad.

Wally laughed, adding, "In a perfect world."

Mr. McGuire's smile disappeared. "Well, maybe you could help us find someone to do the work today?" he suggested. He really wanted this work done as quickly as possible. Mr. McGuire knew how dangerous it could be to have Lizzie and Matt sharing the same space. He still remembered that horrible teething ring incident when Lizzie was five. . . .

Wally smiled. "Yeah . . ." he said slowly, "maybe. You can check around. But if you do decide to hire me, by this afternoon I may have more work scheduled, which means you'd have to wait another week."

Mr. McGuire, still worried about getting the leak fixed as quickly as possible, glanced at his wife for a moment, then turned to Wally. "You're hired."

"Great," Wally said warmly. "Now I just need a check for five, ten, fifteen . . ." He added up the numbers on his clipboard. ". . . One thousand dollars," he said finally. "Then if I don't use it all, I'll give you the rest back."

Mr. McGuire thought for a moment, then walked off to go get the checkbook. Wally looked at Mrs. McGuire.

"Like that's gonna happen," Wally added with a wry smile. He glanced at Mrs. McGuire's newly painted green door, then asked, "Does that green color mean you've got a lot of money?"

That was when Mrs. McGuire decided that the green had to go. "Honey?" she called after her husband. She was going to need some more paint.

* * *

That night, Lizzie had just finished brushing her teeth when she spotted her mother walking down the hallway with a blanket in her arms. "What's that for?" Lizzie asked.

"Matt wants a blanket for his bed," Mrs. McGuire explained.

Lizzie frowned in suspicion. "But I keep my room warm," she protested as she walked into her room. Just then, she was hit with an Arctic wind. Her breath came out in a misty puff. "Why is it so cold in here?"

Matt gestured toward the window. "I like to keep the window open."

"Mom," Lizzie griped, "I don't want to be flash frozen like Matt."

"Okay, Matt," Mrs. McGuire said as she placed the blanket on her son's bed, "you and Lizzie are going to have to cooperate with each other. Each of you is going to have to bend a little bit."

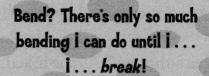 

Bend? There's only so much bending i can do until i . . . i . . . *break!*

"This is *my* room," Lizzie pointed out.

"I know, honey," Lizzie's mom snapped, "but it's *our* house and in times of trouble we stick together. It just so happens that you guys have to stick together in the same room."

Lizzie's eyes flicked over her mom's shoulder to Matt, who made a face and stuck out his tongue. Lizzie narrowed her eyes. I'll show you "times of trouble," Lizzie thought.

"Matt, I saw that," Lizzie's mom said.

Matt's evil grin disappeared. Lizzie had to admit—her mom was impressive. She hadn't even looked in Matt's direction, but she seemed to know exactly what he was doing.

Maybe it was true that mothers had eyes in the backs of their heads. Gross!

"Okay," she said as she walked toward the door. "Good night. Sleep tight. Don't let the bedbugs bite."

Matt smiled at her innocently, and Mrs. McGuire smiled back. Then she turned and walked down the hall.

The moment she was gone, Lizzie turned to Matt. "Okay," Lizzie said sharply. "Here are the *real* rules. You're gonna stay on your bed, and I'm gonna pretend not to notice you. Okay?" She walked over to the window and slammed it shut. "Also: You don't touch my stuff, and I'm gonna pretend not to notice you. And don't speak because then it'll be a whole lot easier for me not to notice you."

"Fine," Matt said casually. Then he looked at the window, adding, "But I want that open."

"No, no, no," Lizzie insisted, "I sleep with

it closed." She crossed over to a machine on her dresser and flipped its switch. The sound of crashing surf filled the room. Lizzie took a deep breath, trying to feel the tranquility entering her body.

Matt made a sour face. "What is *that*?"

Lizzie's eyes snapped open. Okay, she thought, so far, this is so *not* tranquil. "It's my sound soother. The sound of the ocean relaxes me."

Matt leaned over and flipped off the soother. "Oh, yeah?" he said. "Well it makes me seasick." He clicked on a fan, sending cool air whirling through the room.

Lizzie glared at him. "I don't sleep with that on at night."

"I'll burn up," Matt insisted.

I should be so lucky, Lizzie thought. "Well, I'm sorry, take your blanket off."

Matt looked horrified at the suggestion.

"I'll freeze." He ran over to the window and pulled down the shade.

Lizzie ran after him. Wow, Matt's ability to annoy is really reaching new levels, she thought. "I sleep with that open so I can see the moon." She leaned over and yanked up the shade.

"So, that's the howling noise I've been hearing at night," Matt cracked as he reached for the shade. "I want it down."

Not. Happening, Lizzie thought. "Up," she said, pulling at the shade.

"Down," Matt insisted, pulling the shade down.

"No, up!"

"Down!"

"You two had better zip it!" Mr. McGuire shouted from the other side of the wall. "And go to sleep or I'll make you both sleep on the floor."

Suddenly, the shade zipped up by itself. Okay, so that problem's solved, Lizzie thought. But I have a horrible feeling that this isn't over.

Sure enough, five minutes later, Matt turned on his "night-light"—which was really a whirling multicolored disco ball. Then he got up and closed the door and jumped into bed.

"I don't sleep with a night-light," Lizzie said through gritted teeth. She hauled herself out of bed, flipped off the night-light, and opened the door. "And I like the door open." She crawled back into bed.

"I can't sleep with the door open," Matt said. He got up and shut the door, then turned the night-light back on and jumped back into bed.

This went on for quite a while . . . Lizzie got up, pulled up the shade (which Matt had yanked down), and got back into bed. Then Matt pulled the shade down again and got back into bed. Lizzie turned off the fan. Matt turned it on. Lizzie closed the window, and Matt opened it again.

I should sell Matt as a device to annoy people to death, Lizzie thought. Maybe the government would like to buy him.

Lizzie got up, turned the night-light off, and opened the door—and came face-to-face with her dad. His hair was sticking straight up. And he didn't look happy.

"Not. Another. Word," Mr. McGuire growled.

Lizzie gulped and whispered, "Okay." She hadn't seen her dad this mad since Matt tried that "experiment" with the lawn mower and Mr. McGuire's best suit.

Lizzie decided she'd better lay low for a while. She'd get even with Matt . . . later.

CHAPTER FOUR

*T*hud! *Thud! Thud!*

Wally was banging away at the pipes.

"I have got to get some sleep tonight," Mr. McGuire said the next morning as he sat slumped at the dining table, bleary-eyed. Mrs. McGuire sat next to him, looking equally exhausted. First, there had been the endless fighting between Lizzie and Matt, and now . . . this.

Thud! Thud! Thud!

Mrs. McGuire stared up at the ceiling, the source of the hammering. "What time did he start?" she asked.

Mr. McGuire sighed. "Six."

"Okay, I'm thinking about painting the door orange," Mrs. McGuire said, trying to ignore the hammering, which sounded so loud that it seemed to be coming from inside her skull. "What do you think?"

Mr. McGuire looked at her from under heavy eyelids. "Knock, knock," he said.

Mrs. McGuire smiled. "Who's there?"

"Orange."

"Orange who?"

"Orange you gonna get awful sick of an orange door?" Mr. McGuire asked.

Mrs. McGuire chuckled as Lizzie and Matt staggered into the kitchen. Lizzie had to stifle a yawn. She had been up all night, too, arguing with Matt. "Mom, Dad—Matt kept me up all night," she complained. "He talks in his sleep. It is so creepy."

"I don't talk in my sleep," Matt insisted.

Lizzie scoffed. "Like you would know."

"Mom, Lizzie turned off my alarm," Matt complained.

"I don't like alarms," Lizzie explained, exasperated. "They wake me up."

Mrs. McGuire stared at her daughter, dubiously.

"I like it when you wake me up gently," Lizzie elaborated.

"Oh . . . that's so sweet . . ." Mrs. McGuire smiled, then seemed to change her mind. "Wait a minute. You guys, you kept *us* up all night last night."

"It was his fault!" Lizzie cried, pointing at Matt. "He kept bothering me, Mom."

"I never bothered you," Matt said. "I was just trying to make the room comfortable."

"Okay, enough!" Mr. McGuire barked. "Go get ready for school."

Lizzie glared at Matt as they started out of the room. For once, school won't be so bad, she thought. At least it will help me escape from Matt for a few hours!

"How's it coming?" Mr. McGuire asked as Wally walked into the dining room.

Wally grinned and folded his arms across his chest. "Pretty good, actually," he said.

A chunk of plaster dropped from the ceiling, landing on the table with a crash.

Wally stared at the plaster for a moment. "I think I'm going to need a bigger deposit."

And i think i'm gonna be stuck with Matt forever. Mom and Dad brought him into this world. Why can't they get him out of mine?

"I know we're supposed to be supporting Ms. Dew," Gordo said as Lizzie squirted paint into an aluminum tray, "but I don't think that we need to be *practicing* making *handprints*."

Miranda and Gordo followed Lizzie as she carried the paint over to an easel arranged with blank white paper.

"Well, Matt kept me up all night," Lizzie confessed. "So handprints is about all I can handle."

"Oh, so, how's the room-sharing thing going?" Miranda wanted to know.

Lizzie glared at her. Need you ask? she wondered.

Miranda raised her eyebrows. "Oh . . ." she said knowingly, "that good."

Just then, Kate's voice rang out nearby. "Oh, Tudgeman?" Kate sang sweetly to Larry. "You got a little something right here . . ." Kate pointed to her nose.

Larry swiped at his nose with his paint-covered hand. "Here?" he asked, smearing paint across his face.

Kate shook her head. "No," she said in her fake-sweet voice, "over here . . ." She pointed to her cheek, and Larry swiped again.

Kate kept at it. "Kind of over here . . ." Larry smudged more paint on his chin. "No, no . . . over there a little . . ."

Finally, Larry's face was totally covered in gooey paint.

"There," Kate said. "You got it."

Larry grinned. "Thanks, Kate." He turned to Ethan Craft, who was standing behind him. "She digs me," Larry said suavely.

Lizzie shook her head in disbelief. How does Kate even think these things up? Lizzie wondered. Does she plan them all out the night before, in her *Book of Evil*?

Lizzie hated having art with Kate. Then

again, Lizzie thought, at least Ethan is in this class. Ethan was by far the hottest guy in school, and the subject of about eighty percent of Lizzie and Miranda's phone conversations.

Ethan looked over at Larry. "Hey, Tudgeman," he said, pointing to his face. "You got stuff all over your face. It's like here," Ethan said, smearing paint on his own forehead, "and there, and there, and there and there . . ." In about five seconds, Ethan's face was as completely covered with paint as Larry's. Ethan laughed as Larry ducked behind his easel. "I can't believe you fell for that," he said, grinning. Ethan then turned to Lizzie and Miranda. "Ladies," he said smoothly as he ran his paint-smeared hands through the gorgeous hair that topped off his oblivious head.

Miranda giggled while Gordo shook his head. "You know, the scary thing is he's probably going to be very successful at politics."

"Hey, I'd vote for him," Lizzie said brightly. "Even with paint in his hair, he still looks perfect."

"Which means he'll be putting his handprints with all the perfect hair people," Miranda pointed out. "Unlike us, with no place to go."

"Hey, you know what?" Lizzie said suddenly. "Forget about what Kate says, and what Tudgeman says. We're gonna find a group to put our handprints with."

"Oh, very good handprints, Lizzie!" Ms. Dew singsonged as she walked past Lizzie's easel. She clapped in excitement. "Yes."

Lizzie looked at her teacher confusedly. "Uh, thanks, Ms. Dew."

Okay, Lizzie thought as she watched her teacher walk away. Clearly, *I'm* not the only one with problems.

* * *

"This could work," Gordo said as he led Miranda and Lizzie toward the basketball players' locker room. "We like sports. I'm sure the basketball team will let us put our prints with theirs."

Just as the words were out of his mouth, basketball players began pouring from the locker room, nearly pounding the three friends into the floor.

"Out of the way, freaks!" one of the players shouted as he and his teammates trotted off.

"Okay," Miranda said, pursing her lips, "maybe we should start with the geeks."

Lizzie stared at the nerdalicious crowd gathered around the small table where two boys sat staring at a chessboard. It was perfectly silent. Even Miranda and Gordo didn't say a peep as they stood there, watching the chess-board as if it held the secrets of the universe.

Lizzie leaned toward Gordo. "Why don't they move something?" she whispered.

"It's chess," Gordo whispered back. "It takes concentration."

"Maybe they need motivation," Miranda suggested. She took a step forward and shouted, "Go, team, go! Come on! Move that king! Yeah!" She clapped wildly as the chess geeks glared at her.

Lizzie gulped. I never thought it could happen, Lizzie thought, but it looks like the geeks are even out of our league.

Pretty soon the three friends were being ousted from the Chess Club. "Okay, okay," Gordo said as the geeks kept shoving, "all right, we're going."

"I didn't want to put our handprints with theirs anyway," Miranda huffed.

Lizzie sighed. "What's next?"

Gordo shrugged. "Drama club?"

Okay, Lizzie thought, nodding. Drama club—how bad could it be?

Lizzie, Miranda, and Gordo found the room marked with a sign that read "Drama Club Meeting Today" and tiptoed inside. Students in black clothes were scattered around the front of the room. Lizzie did her best to look inconspicuous in her canary-yellow hippie shirt.

Two students were at the front of the room, obviously rehearsing a scene.

"I just wanted to say," the girl said dramatically, "that as I watched you and listened to you, I became you. I then felt I knew you."

Wow, Lizzie thought, she's a real drama queen.

"Of course you did . . ." the guy replied in

a theatrical voice, "because I am what you feel."

Lizzie, Gordo, and Miranda burst into applause. That was amazing! Lizzie thought. These guys are fabulous actors.

The drama queen scowled at Lizzie. "Excuse me?" she snapped. "We're trying to have a personal conversation here."

Lizzie grimaced. "Oh!" she said quickly as the drama monarchs strutted off, "I knew that!" Actually, she thought to herself, I can't believe they were having a real conversation and not just rehearsing lines from a bad European art film! She looked around the room. Everyone was staring at them. "We're leaving immediately."

"Take it easy!" Gordo said as a couple of Drama Groupies shoved the friends out the door.

"I said I'm sorry," Miranda griped to the tough girl who had tossed her out.

Lizzie took a deep breath and straightened her clothes. "That went well."

"Yeah," Miranda said in a bored voice, "so what's next?"

"Hey!" Gordo said, pointing toward the end of the hallway. A large banner read: CHEERLEADER PRACTICE TODAY.

What the heck, Lizzie thought as she and her friends headed toward the sign. At this point, we've got nothing to lose but our dignity.

It was only a matter of seconds before Lizzie and her friends were tossed out of cheerleader practice.

"Okay, that was vicious," Miranda said as a couple of girls from the cheer squad actually tossed pom-poms at them.

Gordo stared down at his vintage bowling shirt and khaki pants. "I like my clothes."

"That's it," Lizzie said sadly. "Nobody wants us be a part of their group."

it's not a Mural of Togetherness, it's a Mural of Make Lizzie Feel Like a Loser.

Well, if it *is* there to make me feel like a loser, Lizzie thought miserably, this mural is definitely working.

CHAPTER FIVE

Mrs. McGuire stood back to admire her door. She had read once that everyone liked blue. And it was a pretty color. Satisfied, she started to close it, but just then Wally walked inside with a bucket and some tools. He looked at the door for a moment.

"Uh-huh," Wally said. "Blue. Kinda sad." He walked off.

"Blue?" Mr. McGuire asked as he stepped into the foyer and caught sight of the door.

"Yeah," Mrs. McGuire said quickly. "Blue. Peaceful."

Mr. McGuire nodded slowly. "It's a little sad, isn't it?"

Just then, Lizzie and Matt barged through the door, shouting "Hi, Mom! Hi, Dad." Their feet thundered on the stairs as they ran up to the room they were now sharing—the one Lizzie had started thinking of as a prison cell.

"Hi, guys!" Mrs. McGuire said warmly. "I think it's peaceful," she said to her husband.

Mr. McGuire lifted his eyebrows and stared up at Lizzie's room. "Not for long."

A scream tore through the house.

Matt and Lizzie came barreling down the stairs.

"Mom, Dad," Lizzie said breathlessly, "somebody has taken everything out of my room!"

"My Weird Al poster is gone!" Matt wailed.

"Relax," Mr. McGuire said. "I put everything in the garage. I do have *this* for you." He reached into the hall closet and pulled out two sleeping bags. He handed one to each of the kids.

Lizzie stared at the sleeping bag, confused. "What is this?"

"Your beds," Mr. McGuire explained. "This week while Matt's room is being repaired and until you two can get along, you'll be sleeping in those."

"You've got to be kidding me," Lizzie said.

Mr. McGuire smiled. "Nope."

Lizzie narrowed her eyes at her father and let out a growl. Then she and Matt stomped upstairs with their new "beds."

Mrs. McGuire stared up at her husband. "You took away all their stuff?"

"I have a plan," Mr. McGuire assured her.

Lizzie chucked her sleeping bag down the stairs.

Mrs. McGuire ignored the flying camping gear. "I am so looking forward to hearing this," she said.

"Well, I just figured if I took away all of the stuff they're fighting over, there'll be nothing left to fight about and they'll just have to work out their problems together," Mr. McGuire explained.

"Wow. That's very forceful of you," Mrs. McGuire said.

Mr. McGuire grinned proudly. "Yeah?"

"Yeah," Mrs. McGuire said, impressed. She linked her arm though her husband's. "I like it," she said, smiling.

"This is all your fault," Lizzie said. It was late, and she was lying flat on her back on the floor in her empty room, wrapped up in a stupid, ugly, uncomfortable sleeping bag. And it was all thanks to Matt and the stupid pipe that stupidly broke in his stupid room.

"My fault?" Matt repeated. "I didn't make the pipe burst."

Lizzie ignored him. She didn't care if what her brother said was true—it didn't help the problem she was having right now, which was that she was seriously uncomfortable. "I want my bed back."

"I want my night-light," Matt added.

"Well, I want my sound soother," Lizzie put in. How am I supposed to get any beauty rest with the noise of pineapple-head's jabber, instead of my relaxing ocean waves, she thought. This isn't getting me anywhere, she realized. "Listen, worm, we're not gonna get anything back if we keep arguing. So, we have to stop."

Matt snorted. "Like *that's* gonna happen."

"Well," Lizzie said slowly, "we don't have to actually stop arguing, we just have to convince Dad that we've stopped."

"Oh, I see," Matt said in his craftiest voice. "Fool our parents . . . I like it."

"I thought you would," Lizzie said.

"Wait," Matt said suddenly, "we don't have to, you know, hug or anything—do we?"

Lizzie made a face. "Ewww! No!"

Just then, Lizzie's dad popped his head into the room. "Are you guys arguing again?"

"Why, no, Father," Matt said in a syrupy voice. "Without our things here to distract us, we've really gotten to know each other." Matt threw his arm around Lizzie's shoulder.

"Yeah," Lizzie added, grinning. "And like each other."

Matt nodded sincerely. "We've really learned our lesson."

"Really?" Mr. McGuire smiled, clearly pleased with himself. "Well, I'm impressed. I think maybe you guys are ready to get your stuff back."

"You think so?" Lizzie asked hopefully.

"Well," Matt put in, "Father does know best."

Mr. McGuire smiled. "I love seeing you two like this. I'll be right back."

Lizzie turned to Matt the moment her Dad hurried away. "'Father?'" she griped, imitating Matt. "What's with the 'Father' thing?"

"'Like each other?'" Matt retorted, quoting Lizzie. "Don't you think that's a bit over the top?"

Lizzie rolled her eyes. "Matt, it's *Dad*," she explained. "It's not like we were trying to fool Mom or anything."

Matt thought for a moment. "True," he admitted.

Lizzie and Matt flopped back into their sleeping bags.

This is going to be a long night, Lizzie thought.

CHAPTER SIX

Lizzie sat at the table next to Matt, eating her cereal. Mr. McGuire was sitting with them, drinking coffee and reading the paper. There was something about the way Matt chewed his food that really bugged Lizzie, but she made an effort not to show it. She and Matt had Dad convinced that they were buddy-buddy. Lizzie didn't want to be the one to blow their cover.

And if Matt blows it, Lizzie thought as she munched her cereal, he will be some serious dead meat.

Matt spoke up just as Mrs. McGuire walked into the kitchen. "Elizabeth?" Matt asked ever-so-sweetly.

"Yes, Matthew?"

Mr. McGuire looked up and saw his wife standing behind Lizzie and Matt. He gave her a huge self-satisfied grin and gestured toward the kids, filled with obvious pride that his brilliant plan had succeeded so well.

"Would you like me to help you carry your books to the bus stop, Elizabeth?" Matt asked.

"Why, Matthew," Lizzie said brightly, "that would be wonderful. Thank you."

Mrs. McGuire rolled her eyes as Lizzie and Matt picked up their stuff and got ready to go.

"Uh-oh," Matt said under his breath as he turned around and caught sight of his mom, who was smiling at them knowingly. "She spotted us."

Lizzie's stomach dropped. Mom. There was

no way she would fall for their "I Just Love My Sibling" routine. "Just run," Lizzie whispered. "Run, run, run, run." Lizzie and Matt beat it out of there.

"See that, honey?" Mr. McGuire said proudly as the kids dashed off. "My plan is working."

Mrs. McGuire shook her head. "Your plan is *not* working," she informed him. "They're not getting along."

"But . . ." Mr. McGuire protested. "They . . ."

"Honey," Mrs. McGuire said patiently, "they're pretending to get along so they can get their stuff back."

Mr. McGuire's face fell. "I knew that," he said.

Mrs. McGuire went back to painting her door. Yellow. Bright, sunny, cheerful yellow. This was it—the perfect color. She was just finishing up as Wally walked down the stairs.

"I've got to buy some new shoes," Wally said to Mrs. McGuire. "These got wet up there. I'll just add it to the bill." Wally looked up at the door. "Yellow? That reminds me of when I was a kid. I had this little baby yellow chick," he said. "He was so sweet."

Mrs. McGuire stared after Wally as he walked out the door, wondering what it was about the colors she chose that seemed to bring out the weird in people.

Suddenly, Wally poked his head back into the room. "He used to go . . . Cheap, cheap, cheap!" Wally cracked up as he left.

"You know, it's supposed to be the sun!" Mrs. McGuire called after him. "You know, bright! Like a new day!"

Mrs. McGuire sighed. Clearly, this yellow *was* going to mean a new day—a new day of painting the door a different color.

CHAPTER SEVEN

"You made it through a whole week with Matt in your room?" Miranda stared at Lizzie in admiration as they walked down the hallway together.

"Let me guess," Gordo said. "While you were sleeping he put whipped cream on your hand and tickled your nose with a feather?"

"Well, things were kind of rocky at first," Lizzie admitted, "but, you know, bottom line is, we're family, and when tough times come around, we have to stick together."

Gordo gave Lizzie a curious look. "You guys really got along?"

Lizzie gaped at him. "Got along?" Is Gordo losing it? she wondered. But then she thought about it for a moment, and she realized that it was true . . . in a way. "I guess we did get along. We kinda had to act like we liked each other to survive Dad's attempt at child psychology." Okay, so they had just been pretending. Still—Lizzie had to give Matt props. He had been convincing. "Matt's a pretty good actor, though."

"Well," Miranda said with a wry smile, "I wish we could pretend to be part of some group, so we'd have someplace to put our handprints."

Gordo shrugged. "Let's just face it. Despite however many different groups of people there are here, we're just not going to belong to any of them."

Lizzie sighed. "I guess you're right."

"It's mural day, it's mural day!" Ms. Dew called as she ran past in a frenzy. "I hope you all remembered to bring your hands."

"I think maybe she meant it that time," Gordo said.

Lizzie nodded, thinking, maybe she did.

The three friends walked into the courtyard. Everyone was standing around in his or her little clique. The Drama Groupies were in the corner, geeks and Mathletes at the far end of the wall, cheerleaders at the center.

"No!" Kate barked as one of the cheerleaders reached toward the wall with a paint-smeared hand. "I already decided that we're going to put our prints in a pyramid. And Tiffany, you have really stubby fingers, so put your print somewhere where no one will notice."

"Hey," Larry announced to the geeks, "I

have an excellent idea." He held up his hand with the fingers divided into a Vulcan V and left a martian-green print on the wall.

"Spock would be proud," Larry announced.

Ethan walked up to Ms. Dew, frowning. "Ms. Dew, I've got a problem."

"Oh, thank you so much for trusting me enough to share it with me," Ms. Dew said eagerly.

Ethan stared at her. "Yeah," he said, "Whatever. But see, it's like this. I keep on trying to do a thumbs-up." Ethan made a fist with his thumb sticking up and tried to press it against the wall. Unfortunately, he did it straight-on so that his knuckles got in the way. "But the wall won't let me," Ethan explained. "You think I should try with my other hand?" He pressed harder.

Lizzie and Miranda exchanged looks. Okay,

so we aren't into Ethan for his mind, Lizzie thought. Lucky for us.

"You know what?" Miranda said. "I'm okay with not being in any of the groups."

"Yeah," Lizzie admitted, "me, too. And when I think about it, the only group I want to be in is standing right next to me."

"Oh, look, there's a spot right there." Gordo pointed to a high place on the wall. "Let's make our move."

Lizzie took her tray of pink paint, Miranda took her red, and Gordo took his hunter green, and they headed over to the wall.

When they were finished, their handprints were there in a row. Together. Like always.

CHAPTER EIGHT

"That's it," Mrs. McGuire said as she stared at her freshly painted door. "That's the color I've been searching for."

Wally overheard her as he walked down the stairs. "How many colors did you go through till you found this one?" he asked.

"A few," Mrs. McGuire admitted.

Wally stood back to admire the door. "Not bad. If you ever need a job, you can work for me."

Mrs. McGuire smiled. "Thank you," she

said, although she didn't think she would feel like painting any more doors in the near future.

"That's for you," Wally said as he handed her an envelope and walked out the door.

Mrs. McGuire looked down at the envelope, surprised. "Oh." She pulled it open just as Mr. McGuire walked into the room.

"Was that the construction guy?" Mr. McGuire asked.

"Yeah. Look at this." Mrs. McGuire took some money out of the envelope—the refund on the huge amount of money they had put down as a deposit. Truthfully, neither of them had ever expected to get anything back, so this was a real windfall. "Two dollars and forty-three cents," Mrs. McGuire announced.

"Now that's a shock," Mr. McGuire said with a wry smile. "Hey," he said, looking at the door. "I like it."

Mrs. McGuire nodded. White. Clean,

crisp, simple white. So what if it was exactly where they'd started? "Yeah," she admitted, "I think I do, too."

"See you, honey." Mr. McGuire grabbed the two dollars and headed out the door.

"You don't want the change?" Mrs. McGuire asked as she held up the rest of the dough.

Mr. McGuire grinned.

Now all they had to do was decide how to spend all that money.

"This is so messy," Lizzie said as she wiped the paint from her hands with a paper towel.

"Yeah," Miranda agreed, "but it was a cool way of getting everyone out of school for half the day."

"Hey," Gordo said, "we ought to go back and sign our names next to our handprints."

Lizzie nodded—good idea. That Gordo, he's always thinking.

The three friends turned back to the wall, which was covered in a spectrum of hand-prints.

Miranda frowned. "Which ones are ours?"

Lizzie shook her head. There were so many prints, all blending together, that it was impossible to tell whose were whose. *I guess that was the idea all along,* Lizzie realized as she stared at the wall. *And I guess Ms. Dew isn't as nutty as she seems.*

You know, after seeing Ms. Dew's Mural of Togetherness, the whole thing about which group put their handprints where didn't matter much. 'Cause when you look at it, all of the prints kinda blend together in a group that's just . . . us.

Lizzie and her friends walked away from the wall arm in arm. She'd learned over these past few days that whether it was an annoying brother at home or a clique at school, she had more in common with some people than she would like to think. The thing was, this didn't upset her at all—it actually made her feel, well, pretty great. She just hoped her parents didn't expect her to be hugging her little bro' anytime soon. Some lines, she thought, should never be crossed . . . And she knew Matt would agree!

Don't close the book on Lizzie yet!
Here's a sneak peek at the next
Lizzie McGuire story. . . .

Adapted by Jasmine Jones
Based on the series created by Terri Minsky
Based on a teleplay
by Douglas Tuber & Tim Maile.

"I was watching this spy movie last night,"
Lizzie McGuire's best friend David "Gordo"
Gordon said as he followed Lizzie and her

other best friend, Miranda Sanchez, into the McGuires' hallway. "And it got me thinking—why do supervillains always want to take over the world?"

Lizzie thought for a minute. That was the thing about Gordo—you could always count on him to come up with a random question that was actually a pretty good, if not weird, point. "Well," Lizzie said, "I think it would be kind of cool to rule the world." She smiled at Miranda. "I mean, you could meet any celebrity you wanted."

Actually, Lizzie thought, there could be a lot of fringe benefits.

i could pass a new law making Ethan Craft worship me.

If ever there were a reason to take over the world, Ethan Craft was *so* it. Ethan was in Lizzie's grade at Hillridge Junior High, and both she and Miranda agreed that he was like dry ice—totally cool and totally hot at the same time. Hanging with him would be the cornerstone of Lizzie's reign as Imperial Empress of Planet Earth!

And i guess i could feed starving people or something. But Ethan Craft would be Priority Number One.

Gordo shook his head. "You'd have to be in charge of *everything*," he pointed out, gesturing wildly. "What if the electricity went out in Stockholm? Or there's a mud slide in Argentina? Or Thailand's being infested with aphids—I mean, what do you do?"

Lizzie furrowed her brow. "I never thought of it that way, Gordo," she admitted. Sheesh, I had enough trouble picking out this bandanna this morning, Lizzie thought as she flipped the ends of her pink sparkly head scarf over her shoulders. I would totally not want to have to add "Deal with Thailand aphids" to my To Do list.

"Well, luckily, I don't want to rule the world," Miranda said with a grin as she folded her arms across her chest. "I want to be a singer on a cruise ship."

Lizzie smiled dubiously at her friend, who was wearing a typical-Miranda funky outfit—dark red streaks in her jet-black hair, sideways sun visor, black pants, red shirt that read "Love," and chunky black shoes. Right, Lizzie thought, I can just see Miranda in some gold lamé dress singing "Love Will Keep Us Together" for the shuffleboard set. Give me the aphids any day.

"Hey, kids," Mrs. McGuire said as she walked into the kitchen with an enormous box covered in pastel wrapping paper. "Lizzie—you got a package from Gammy McGuire," Lizzie's mom said, as she handed the box over to her daughter.

"Excellent," Lizzie said with little excitement. "My grandmother can't remember when my birthday is," she explained to her best friends, rolling her eyes, "so she just sends me stuff every couple months, just to make sure." Of course, the stuff is always lame, Lizzie thought. Once she sent me a sweater with a unicorn on it that was so ugly it nearly ruined my life.

She ripped open the box.

"Ooh, maybe it's that scarf you want!" Miranda said eagerly. "Or those cool rhinestone sunglasses! Or that jewelry box!"

Lizzie pulled the gift out of the box. Her grandmother had sent her a board game.

"'Dwarflord: The Conquest,'" Lizzie read aloud. She was not impressed.

Miranda grimaced, as though she had caught a whiff of something foul. "Or it could, you know, *reek*."

"'The game of dragon monarchs and dwarf warriors,'" Lizzie went on, reading from the lid of the game. She sighed. Gammy's gifts just get worse and worse, she thought.

"Like I said . . ." Miranda put in.

Lizzie kept reading as she headed into the kitchen. "'Imagine you're an exiled Dwarflord, seeking to reclaim your kingdom, stolen by an evil wizard and guarded by his dragon slaves.'"

Imagine you're an exiled board game, doomed to become one with a landfill, Lizzie thought as she lifted the trash can lid.

"Hey!" Lizzie's mother gave her a disapproving frown as she grabbed the game out of

Lizzie's hand. "You're not throwing your gift away."

Gordo looked at Mrs. McGuire as though she were crazy. "Why not?" Gordo demanded. "Didn't you hear about the Dwarflords?"

Mrs. McGuire looked at the ceiling in frustration. "I want you to play it at least one time," she said to Lizzie, "and then, if you don't like it, we're going to donate it to charity."

Lizzie sighed. Donate it to charity? she thought. Haven't those poor children suffered enough? But she knew that there was no point in arguing with her mother.

"Fine, I'll play it." Lizzie turned to her friends. "C'mon, Gordo, Miranda, let's get this over with."

"Oh," Miranda said quickly, pursing her lips, "I gotta go home and clean fish." She pointed at the door. "See my dad went fishing so I have to go home and . . ." Miranda raised her eyebrows, obviously trying to think of something that would clinch her excuse. ". . . gut them."

Lizzie narrowed her eyes. And I thought that *I* was a lousy liar, Lizzie said to herself as she watched her friend squirm. She looked at Gordo.

"Yeah, and I'm going to go home and try to grow a mustache," Gordo threw in quickly. "I've been meaning to."

"Miranda, I let you borrow my blue top, and you got deviled eggs all over it, okay?" Lizzie snapped. "You owe me."

"All right, all right . . ." Miranda grumbled.

"And Gordo, if you don't play, I'll tell everyone what you did at Dakota Himmelfarb's Fourth of July party," Lizzie said, lifting her eyes knowingly.

Gordo looked blank.

"You know," Lizzie prompted, "with the mustard—"

"Hey, what are we wasting time yakking for?" Gordo said quickly. "Let's play Dwarflord!"

Lizzie nodded. She hated to stoop to blackmail, but if it was the only way to get Gordo to play Dwarflord, she guessed she had to go with it. Besides, I'm glad that mustard thing finally paid off, she thought, then shuddered. Although it was really gross.

Still, it wasn't half as gross as Dwarflord.

Dear Gammy McGuire,
Thank you so much for the cool present. Next time, please send cash.

"Okay, Lizzie." Miranda scanned the rule book. At least, I think it's the rule book, Lizzie thought as she gaped at the huge tome. It's so thick, it looks like it could be the Los Angeles phone book. The game board was spread out before them, covered in playing pieces. This game may not be fun, Lizzie thought, but it sure is complicated. "You're in the Seventh Realm of Discovery, so you have to roll the Dream Dice, and the toe-bone of Rumblepeter Goblin-beater," Miranda explained.

Lizzie rolled her eyes. "But I thought I could get out of the Seventh Realm of Discovery by getting a wish-feather from a mooncat."

"Let's see . . ." Miranda said as she flipped through the huge book. "Lodestones . . . troll-blessings . . . oh, here it is. It says if you don't roll the toe-bone, you have to cross the Bridge of Ultimate Darkness and spend your wish-feather on Insanity Syrup." Miranda looked up, completely confused.

I think I already drank some Insanity Syrup,

Lizzie thought miserably. That's the only logi-
cal reason that I would be playing this game.

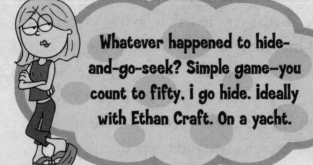

Whatever happened to hide-
and-go-seek? Simple game—you
count to fifty. I go hide. Ideally
with Ethan Craft. On a yacht.

"We've been playing this game for twenty
minutes now, okay?" Lizzie said impatiently.
"Gammy McGuire's gift has been . . ." Lizzie
searched for the right word. ". . . enjoyed."

Miranda nodded.

"You guys just want to quit 'cause I'm winning," Gordo said.

Miranda gaped at him. "You are?" she said
as she stared down at the rule book and flipped
through the pages. "How can you tell?"

Gordo shrugged. "Well, I've acquired the Thirteen Skulls," he said with a knowing grin, ". . . and you know what that means."

"No, I really don't," Lizzie told him, shaking her head. "Nor do I care."

Is Gordo serious? Lizzie wondered. I'm sitting here thinking that Dwarflord puts the bore in board game, and he's talking magic skulls?

"Well, I can trade them in for a Shapeshifting Button," Gordo explained. "I turn into the Dragon Monarch—then I need to get an Inferno Robe and a Smoke Shield."

Miranda looked over at Lizzie. "Mall?" she suggested.

"You bet." Lizzie nodded and hauled herself out of her chair.

Lizzie and Miranda headed for the door.

"All right, all right—" Gordo surrendered. "I'll come."

Sorry! That's the end of the sneak
peek for now. But don't go nuclear!
To read the rest, all you have to do
is look for the next title in the
Lizzie McGuire series—

Wake up.
Go to school.
Save the world.

Will   Irma   Taranee   Cornelia   Hay Lin

0-7868-1728-3   0-7868-1729-1   0-7868-1730-5   0-7868-1731-3   0-7868-1732-1   0-7668-1795-X

Groove to the sound of all your favorite shows

Disney Channel Soundtrack Series

Disney's
Kim Possible
TV Soundtrack

The Cheetah Girls
TV Soundtrack

Lizzie McGuire
TV Soundtrack

Pixel Perfect
Soundtrack

Also, look for...

- ### *The Proud Family* TV Series Soundtrack
- ### *That's So Raven* TV Series Soundtrack

Collect them all!